ANGELA'S
CHRISTMAS
WISH

Adapted by Leigh Olsen
from the screenplay written by Damien O'Connor
Based on the characters created by Frank McCourt
Illustrated by Brown Bag Films

Simon Spotlight
New York   London   Toronto   Sydney   New Delhi

SIMON SPOTLIGHT

An imprint of Simon & Schuster Children's Publishing Division

1230 Avenue of the Americas, New York, New York 10020

This Simon Spotlight hardcover edition September 2021

For information about special discounts for bulk purchases,

please contact Simon & Schuster Special Sales at 1-866-506-1949 or business@simonandschuster.com.

Manufactured in United States of America 0821 LAK

2 4 6 8 10 9 7 5 3 1

ISBN 978-1-6659-0377-6

ISBN 978-1-6659-0378-3 (ebook)

When Angela was little more than a baby, her dad left Ireland on a big ship. She and her mother; her older brothers, Tom and Pat; and her baby sister, Aggie, all came to the shipyard to say goodbye.

Angela waved at her dad as he stood on the back deck of the ship. She wished he didn't have to take that new job in Australia. She knew she would miss him all the time—most especially at Christmas.

Two years later, on Christmas Eve, Angela was at church. She spoke to Baby Jesus as he lay in his manger. "Mr. McGinty's cow is having a baby!" she told him. "Mom says he's worried he can't get a cow doctor on Christmas. Maybe you could have a word upstairs to make sure everything's okay."

"Angela, it's time to go," her mother called from the back of the church.

Angela leaned in and whispered to Baby Jesus. "Mom has been in an odd mood the last few days. She's been cleaning and scrubbing and fussing, and I'm not sure what's the matter!"

Angela waved goodbye. "See you tomorrow at Christmas Mass!" she exclaimed.

At home, Angela's mother got right back to cleaning. "Go on and tidy your room," she told the children, shooing them upstairs.

"But, Mom," said Tom, "it's Christmas Eve. Can't we have a story first?"

Their mother smiled. "Oh, all right," she said. "There's always time for a story."

Everyone gathered around the table. "Once upon a time," she began, "there was a big king and a little pauper. One day, they met a genie. He granted them each one wish.

"The king wished for all the gold in the world, but the pauper said quietly, 'I wish, I wish, I wish . . .'"

The children leaned in close. "What did the pauper wish for?" Angela asked.

But their mother didn't answer. "Years later," she continued, "the king had gone mad with gold. It was in his socks, his boots, and even under his pillow. But the pauper was the happiest man alive! The king pleaded, 'Tell me your wish!' And the pauper smiled. 'All right,' says he, 'I'll tell you . . .'

"The pauper said, 'I wished, I wished, I wished . . .'"
Their mother paused.

"What did he wish for?" Pat pleaded.

She laughed. "Clean your room, and I'll tell you!"

"Mom!" Angela exclaimed.

"Come on—go," their mother said. "We have to get this house shipshape!"

But upstairs, the children didn't feel like cleaning. "Do you think Mom is all right?" Angela asked. "She's been acting funny for days, all rushing and fussing."

"It's the same every Christmas," said Tom. "Mom misses Dad." They all missed him too.

Suddenly, Angela had an idea. When Tom went downstairs, Angela turned to Pat. "Let's get Dad home from Australia!" she said. "It will be the perfect Christmas surprise for Mom."

"I bet we could take a train and be there in an hour!" Pat said.

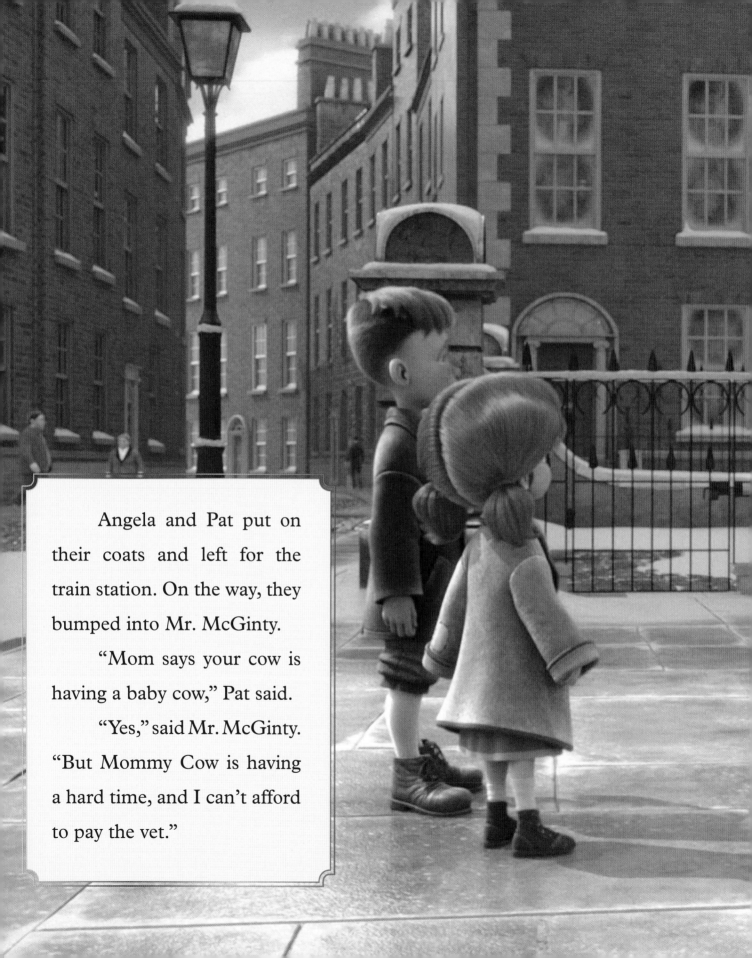

Angela and Pat put on their coats and left for the train station. On the way, they bumped into Mr. McGinty.

"Mom says your cow is having a baby cow," Pat said.

"Yes," said Mr. McGinty. "But Mommy Cow is having a hard time, and I can't afford to pay the vet."

"Will she be all right?" Angela asked.

"God willing, she will," said Mr. McGinty.

"Can we call the baby cow Socks?" Angela asked.

Mr. McGinty chuckled. "Socks the calf it is, Angela," he said as he went on his way.

As soon as Mr. McGinty was out of sight, Angela turned to Pat. "We have to help Socks!"

Once Angela made up her mind, there was no stopping her. She led Pat straight to the vet's house and marched right up the front steps.

Before she could knock, the door swung open. A little girl Angela's age stood there.

"We need the vet to help Mr. McGinty's cow!" blurted Angela.

The little girl's eyes widened. Then she called into the house. "Mother! This is the girl who took Baby Jesus from church!"

The girl's mother looked at Angela and Pat curiously.

"I was just keeping him warm," Angela said sheepishly, explaining why she had taken Baby Jesus from the manger at the church. "It was cold, so I took him home to warm him. And anyway, he is back in the manger at St. Joseph's now."

"Well, then, Dorothy, we'd better invite them in," said the girl's mother.

Inside, Dorothy's father, the vet, was so busy reading the newspaper, he didn't even look up to say hello.

Dorothy's mother brought tea and cake. "Are you looking forward to Christmas?" she asked Angela and Pat.

"We're getting Mom a big surprise," said Pat.

Angela nodded. "We're going on a train to get our dad home from Australia!"

At that, Dorothy's father lowered his paper. "That's simply absurd!" he exclaimed.

Dorothy's mother smiled at Angela and Pat. "Well, I think it's a wonderful idea," she said.

"Daddy," said Dorothy, "Angela has something to ask you."

Dorothy's father peered at Angela. "Mr. McGinty's cow is having a baby," she said nervously. "Can you help?"

The vet thought for a moment. "I'll make you a deal," he said. "Get your father back, and I will help your cow."

"Deal!" said Angela, shaking his hand.

When Angela and Pat left, Dorothy followed them outside. "I can help get your father home!" she exclaimed.

"You can?" said Pat.

"Father was right. You can't take the train to Australia," Dorothy said. "But I know another way."

Dorothy took Angela and Pat to the shipyard—the very same place their father had left from all those years ago. They approached the man in the ticket booth. "Three tickets to Australia, please!" Angela said.

But the man just laughed. "What a funny joke!" he said. Then he closed the window right in their faces!

But Dorothy wasn't going to let that stop them.

"This way!" Dorothy whispered. She climbed on top of a barrel and over a wall into the shipyard. Angela and Pat followed right behind.

Inside, there were shipping crates everywhere—and one huge ship, with smoke billowing out of its smokestack.

Suddenly, the ship let out a huge honk. "All aboard!" shouted the ship's captain.

"We'd better hurry!" said Angela. "The ship's leaving!" She, Pat, and Dorothy raced toward the ship. But at that very moment, the man from the ticket booth spotted them.

"Hey!" he shouted angrily. "Get back here!"

A sailor caught Pat and Dorothy before they could climb aboard. But Angela kept running as fast as she could toward the big ship.

"Get Dad home!" Pat shouted.

Angela made it to the gangplank just in time—or so she thought.

The ship began to pull away from the dock. She was too late.

Angela and Pat were never going to get to Australia now.
"I'm sorry you didn't get your dad home," said Dorothy.

Angela pulled a photo of her father from her pocket, looking at it sadly. "Thanks," she said. She supposed they'd have to spend another Christmas without him.

On the way home, Angela asked to stop at the church. She thought maybe Baby Jesus could help.

Angela walked inside the quiet church and stood in front of him.

"I couldn't get him home, Baby Jesus," she said. "Now we can't give Mom her Christmas surprise."

But Baby Jesus just looked up at her.

When Angela and Pat walked in the door to their house, their mother took one look at them and asked, "What is it?"

"We didn't get your Christmas surprise," said Angela.

"Oh, my darling," said their mother, giving her a hug. "It doesn't matter."

"Would you like to know what the pauper wished for in the story?" their mother asked. The children looked at her, waiting. "He wished to be happy. He could have had anything in the world. But when he looked into his heart, the words just came to him. 'I wish, I wish, I wish . . .'"

"To be happy," Angela finished.

"Try it with me," their mother said. "Listen to what your hearts want."

Tom went first. "I wish, I wish, I wish . . . ," he said. And he pictured his wish coming true.

"I wish, I wish, I wish . . . ," said Pat.

Finally, it was Angela's turn. She closed her eyes. "I wish, I wish, I wish . . ."

Angela opened her eyes.

She couldn't believe what she was seeing.

Her father stood in the doorway of their home, smiling.

"Happy Christmas, everyone," he said.

Angela ran straight into her father's arms.

"Surprise," said Mom, who had known all along.

"I wished for Dad!" said Pat. "He's here!"

"Me too!" said Tom.

"Dada!" cried Aggie.

The children wrapped their father in a warm embrace.

Now that the children's greatest wish had come true, there was one last thing to do. Angela brought her entire family to the vet's house.

"We had a deal," Angela told him. "I get my dad home. You help Mr. McGinty's cow!"

"How on earth did you do that?" he asked. But a deal was a deal. Dorothy gave him his vet bag.

"How did you get your father home?" Dorothy asked.

"I wished," Angela said.

Then Dorothy made her own wish. "I wish, I wish, I wish . . . ," she began, and her wish came true! Her father asked her to come along to help him. They would share a grand adventure!

"Thank you," Dorothy whispered to Angela as she and her father started off for Mr. McGinty's.

On the way home, Angela stopped at the toy shop, where she picked out the perfect Christmas present for Socks the Cow.

The next morning, Angela and her family went to church for Christmas Mass. During the sermon, Angela made sure to wave hello to Baby Jesus on his birthday.

She had a feeling maybe he had something to do with her Christmas surprise after all.

Meanwhile, Mr. McGinty's cow had a healthy baby calf—thanks to a little help from the vet . . . and Dorothy.

Socks especially liked his Christmas present from Angela: four little red socks to keep his hooves warm.

That evening, Angela's father tucked everyone into bed.

He leaned down and kissed Angela on the forehead.

"Happy Christmas, Angela," he said.

"Happy Christmas, Dada," she replied.